The First Men in the Moon

H. G. Wells

It was unreal and fantastic. The strangeness of what we did, the unearthliness of it, was overwhelming. The whole enterprise was mad. And it comes to me that my participation in these amazing adventures was, after all, the purest accident.

I WAS LIVING AT LYMPNE, ENGLAND, NEXT DOOR TO AN ODD LITTLE SCIENTIST NAMED CAVOR. ON 14TH OCTOBER, 1899, I WAS STANDING ON MY VERANDAH WATCHING HIM APPROACH FOR AFTERNOON TEA WHEN SUDDENLY...

CAVOR'S HOUSE IS GOING UP!

THE TREES ABOUT THE BUILDING TORE THEMSELVES TO PIECES AND SPRANG SKYWARDS.

THEN CAME THE WIND.

CAVOR AND I WERE BOTH BLOWN THROUGH THE SCREAMING AIR TOWARDS THE HOUSE.

THEN A BLUISH SHINING SUBSTANCE RUSHED UPWARDS.

AFTER THIS, THE WORST WAS OVER. THE WIND FELL SWIFTLY TILL IT WAS MERELY A GALE.

CAVOR! CAVOR!

A TATTERED OBJECT ROSE FROM THE MUD.

CONGRATULATE ME, BEDFORD! CONGRATULATE ME!

GOOD HEAVENS! WHAT FOR?

I'VE DONE IT! COME, LET'S GO TO YOUR HOUSE AND I'LL EXPLAIN.

WE MANAGED TO REACH THE SHELTER OF AS MUCH ROOF AS WAS LEFT TO ME.

WELL?

I HAVE MADE A SUBSTANCE WHICH CUTS OFF THE FORCE OF GRAVITY.

WHAT?

YOU KNOW THAT THERE ARE SCREENS OF VARIOUS SORTS TO CUT OFF LIGHT OR HEAT. BUT UNTIL TODAY, NOTHING HAD BEEN DISCOVERED WHICH COULD CUT OFF THE GRAVITATIONAL PULL OF THE EARTH.

INCREDIBLE!

UNFORTUNATELY, I MADE THIS SUBSTANCE -- WHICH I CALL CAVORITE -- IN A THIN, WIDE SHEET.

THAT MEANT THAT WHEN THE MANUFACTURE BECAME COMPLETE, JUST NOW, EVERYTHING ABOVE THE SHEET CEASED TO HAVE WEIGHT.

SO THAT'S WHY THE AIR AND THE ROOF ABOVE THE CAVORITE WENT UP WITH SUCH VIOLENCE?

YES. AND WHEN THE AIR AROUND IT PRESSED IN TO TAKE ITS PLACE, IT WAS IN TURN FLUNG UPWARDS.

IF THE CAVORITE ITSELF HAD NOT BEEN SUCKED UP, THE AIR WOULD STILL BE RUSHING UP AND OVER IT, SPOUTING THE ATMOSPHERE OF THE EARTH INTO SPACE!

IT SOUNDS LIKE AN EXTREMELY DANGEROUS INVENTION. WHAT DO YOU PLAN TO DO NOW?

FIND SOME PRACTICAL USE FOR IT -- TRANSPORTATION, PERHAPS.

HOW DO YOU MEAN?

IMAGINE A HOLLOW SPHERE ENAMELLED, AS IT WERE, WITH CAVORITE. IN SUCH A VEHICLE WE COULD TRAVEL INDEFINITELY IN SPACE -- TO THE MOON, PERHAPS!

CONFOUND IT, THE MOON'S A QUARTER OF A MILLION MILES AWAY!

THAT'S NOTHING WHEN YOU'RE TRAVELLING WITH CAVORITE. AFTER ALL, TO GO INTO OUTER SPACE IS NOT ANY WORSE THAN GOING ON A POLAR EXPEDITION.

BUT IF ANYTHING GOES WRONG ON A POLAR EXPEDITION, THERE ARE RELIEF PARTIES. BUT THIS -- IT'S JUST FIRING OURSELVES OFF THE WORLD FOR NOTHING.

CALL IT PROSPECTING. IT ISN'T AS THOUGH YOU WERE CONFINED TO THE MOON.

YOU MEAN...?

THERE'S MARS. IT MIGHT BE PLEASANT TO GO THERE. IT'S TWO HUNDRED MILLION MILES AWAY, AND YOU GO CLOSE BY THE SUN.

My IMAGINATION STARTED TO PICK UP. THE TRANSITION FROM DOUBT TO ENTHUSIASM TOOK NO TIME AT ALL.

BUT THIS IS TREMENDOUS! I WOULD NEVER DREAM OF THIS SORT OF THING.

We ACTED LIKE MEN INSPIRED.

LET'S GET TO WORK ON OUR PLANS THIS VERY NIGHT.

LET'S GET TO WORK RIGHT NOW!

*F*OR MONTHS WE WORKED WITH UNFLAGGING ENTHUSIASM. THE GLASS SPHERE WE HAD ORDERED ARRIVED.

*T*HEN CAME THE STEEL BLINDS. CAVOR HAD DESIGNED THEM TO BE AFFIXED TO THE OUTSIDE OF THE SPHERE AND THEN COATED WITH CAVORITE.

WITH ALL THE BLINDS CLOSED, WE WILL FLY THROUGH SPACE IN A STRAIGHT LINE.

BUT IF WE RAISE ONE OR MORE BLINDS, WE WILL BE ATTRACTED BY ANY HEAVY BODY THAT CHANCES TO BE IN THAT DIRECTION.

AH, THEN WE SHALL BE ABLE TO TACK ABOUT IN SPACE JUST AS WE WISH. GET ATTRACTED TO THIS AND THAT.

EXACTLY.

WHAT PROVISIONS SHALL WE TAKE ON OUR JOURNEY?

WE'LL NEED CONCENTRATED FOODS, CYLINDERS OF OXYGEN, WATER CONDENSERS -- THINGS LIKE THAT.

IT WAS NOT UNTIL THE CAVORITE WAS ALMOST READY THAT I BEGAN TO BE ASSAILED BY DOUBTS.

BUT LOOK HERE, CAVOR, WHAT'S IT ALL FOR?

YOU ARE TIRED. YOU HAD BETTER GO TO BED EARLY.

I DID, BUT MY SLEEP WAS RACKED BY HORRIBLE NIGHTMARES.

THE NEXT MORNING...

I'M NOT GOING. THE THING'S TOO MAD!

I WOULD NOT GO TO THE LABORATORY, BUT INSTEAD SET OFF FOR A WALK. AFTER AN EXCELLENT LUNCH AT AN INN AND A PLEASANT SLEEP IN A SUNNY PLACE, I RETURNED HOME REFRESHED.

WELL, HOW DO YOU FEEL NOW?

I'M COMING. I JUST HAD A CASE OF NERVES.

SPLENDID! WE HAVE ONLY TO HEAT THE CAVORITE, AND WE'LL BE OFF!

A FEW DAYS LATER, ALL WAS READY.

GO ON.

HE CRAWLED IN AFTER ME. WE SCREWED IN THE MANHOLE COVER AND SAT WAITING FOR THE CAVORITE TO COOL AND RELEASE US FROM THE GRAVITATIONAL PULL OF THE EARTH.

THERE CAME A LITTLE JERK, AND IN A MOMENT WE WERE FLYING AS SWIFTLY AS A BULLET UP INTO THE GULF OF SPACE.

LOOK, EVERYTHING IS FLOATING.

OF COURSE. WE ARE CUT OFF FROM ALL EXTERIOR GRAVITATION.

IT WAS THE STRANGEST SENSATION, FLOATING THUS LOOSELY IN SPACE. IT WAS NOT LIKE THE BEGINNING OF A JOURNEY, IT WAS LIKE THE BEGINNING OF A DREAM.

*P*RESENTLY I ROUSED MYSELF.

HOW ARE WE POINTING? WHAT IS OUR DIRECTION?

SOMEWHERE TOWARDS THE MOON, I THINK. LET'S TAKE A LOOK.

*T*HERE CAME A CLICK AND A BLIND IN THE OUTER CASE SNAPPED OPEN TO REVEAL THE BLINDING SPLENDOUR OF THE WANING MOON.

*C*AVOR OPENED THREE MORE BLINDS.

NOW THE GRAVITATION OF THE MOON WILL PULL US TO HER.

*W*E SOON FOUND THAT WE, AS WELL AS OUR BAGGAGE, WERE COMING TO REST ON THE SIDE OF THE SPHERE NEAREST THE MOON.

WE STARED IN FASCINATION.

DO YOU THINK THERE MIGHT BE PEOPLE, OR CREATURES OF SOME SORT DOWN THERE?

IT'S MOST UNLIKELY.

THINK OF THE CONDITIONS ANY SORT OF LIFE WOULD HAVE TO FIT ITSELF TO -- A CLOUDLESS SUN-BLAZE OF A DAY AS LONG AS FOURTEEN OF OURS, AND THEN A FREEZING NIGHT OF EQUAL LENGTH.

ONE CAN IMAGINE SOME INSECT, PERHAPS, THAT COULD BURROW AND HIDE FROM THE LUNAR NIGHT. BUT WE SHALL SOON FIND OUT.

BY THE WAY, WHY DIDN'T WE BRING A GUN?

I DIDN'T THINK WE WOULD NEED ONE. BUT WE SHALL SEE WHEN WE GET THERE.

THEN WE GAVE WAY TO A CURIOUS DROWSINESS, AND IN A STATE THAT WAS NEITHER WAKING NOR SLUMBER, WE FELL SILENTLY AND SWIFTLY TOWARDS THE MOON.

ONE DAY CAVOR SUDDENLY OPENED SIX OF THE BLINDS AND THE GREAT MOUNTAINS AND CRATERS OF THE MOON LEAPED INTO VIEW.

WE'RE NOT FAR NOW.

HE RUSHED ABOUT OPENING AND SHUTTING BLINDS. SOON...

WE'RE GOING TO LAND!

THERE CAME A JAR, AND THEN WE WERE ROLLING OVER AND OVER DOWN A SLOPE.

FINALLY, WE STOPPED WITH A BUMP.

WHY IS IT SO DARK AND COLD?

IT'S NIGHT HERE STILL. WE MUST WAIT FOR DAY TO OVERTAKE US.

I SAT FRETTING IMPATIENTLY UNTIL SUDDEN, SWIFT AND AMAZING, CAME THE LUNAR DAY. THE BRIGHTNESS OF IT STABBED OUR EYES.

T HE MOUNDS OF WHAT LOOKED LIKE SNOW TURNED TO MIST AT THE TOUCH OF A SUNBEAM.

WHY, IT ISN'T SNOW -- IT'S FROZEN AIR!

M IST SWIRLED ABOUT US AS THE HEAT OF THE SUN THAWED THE FROZEN ATMOSPHERE.

F INALLY THE ARCTIC CHARACTER OF THE LAND DISAPPEARED, REVEALING RUSTY-BROWN SPACES OF EARTH.

I STRAINED MY EYES TO SEE BETTER.

CAVOR! THERE ARE LITTLE ROUND OBJECTS OVER THERE THAT LOOK LIKE SEEDS!

*A*S WE WATCHED, FIRST ONE THEN ANOTHER CRACKED AND SENT UP A YELLOWISH-GREEN SHOOT.

LIFE! THERE IS LIFE HERE!

*T*HE PLANTS GREW SO QUICKLY THAT THEY SOON COVERED THE GROUND AS FAR AS THE EYE COULD SEE.

THEY MUST GO THROUGH THEIR WHOLE CYCLE OF GROWTH IN A BRIEF MOON DAY.

IF PLANTS CAN GROW HERE, THERE MUST BE AIR -- AIR THAT WE COULD BREATHE.

YES. LET US FIND OUT.

WE BEGAN TO UNSCREW THE MANHOLE COVER.

SLOWLY, THE AIR OF OUR SPHERE MIXED WITH THE THINNER AIR OF THE MOON.

CAN YOUR LUNGS STAND IT?

YES.

WE RAISED THE COVER. THEN WE CLIMBED UP TO THE MANHOLE, SWUNG OUR LEGS OVER AND DROPPED UPON THE UNTRODDEN SOIL OF THE MOON.

IN FRONT OF US WAS A SORT OF DITCH. CAVOR DREW HIMSELF TOGETHER AND...

SUDDENLY HE WAS THIRTY FEET AWAY!

HOW DID HE DO THAT?

I ALSO JUMPED AND FOUND MYSELF FLYING THROUGH THE AIR.

I LANDED BESIDE HIM IN A STATE OF INFINITE AMAZEMENT.

WHAT IS HAPPENING TO US?

REMEMBER, YOUR WEIGHT HERE IS BARELY A SIXTH OF WHAT IT WAS ON EARTH.

WE MUST EDUCATE OUR MUSCLES TO THIS NEW ATMOSPHERE OR WE'LL SMASH OURSELVES ON THE ROCKS. LET US TRY LEAPING AGAIN.

AFTER ABOUT THIRTY LEAPS WE FOUND WE COULD JUDGE DISTANCES WITH ASSURANCE.

LET'S REST A FEW MINUTES.

WE GAZED ABOUT US.

SEE HOW FAST THE PLANTS HAVE BEEN GROWING! IT MAKES THE TERRAIN LOOK QUITE DIFFERENT.

SUDDENLY A TERRIFYING THOUGHT STRUCK ME.

CAVOR! WHERE IS THE SPHERE?

WE SPRANG UP. IT WAS NOWHERE TO BE SEEN.

*T*HEN WE HEARD A DULL POUNDING COMING FROM BENEATH OUR FEET.

WHAT CAN IT BE?

I DON'T KNOW. THIS IS BEYOND UNDERSTANDING. WE MUST FIND THE SPHERE!

*S*UDDENLY THERE CAME A NEW NOISE.

WHAT IS THAT?

IT SOUNDS LIKE THE BELLOWING OF GREAT BEASTS.

*W*E GAZED, TERRIFIED, AS AN ENORMOUS ANIMAL CAME INTO VIEW.

IT'S A SORT OF COW, I THINK.

A GIGANTIC MOON-CALF!

THEN...

CAVOR! LOOK!

BEHIND THE MOON-CALF AND APPARENTLY HERDING IT CAME A STRANGE LOOKING CREATURE.

WE WATCHED UNTIL IT DISAPPEARED FROM SIGHT.

IT LOOKS RATHER LIKE A LARGE ANT.

IT MUST BE A MOON-MAN -- A SELENITE. LET'S FIND THAT SPHERE!

WE CREPT STEALTHILY UNTIL WE CAME TO A HUGE FLAT AREA WHICH SUDDENLY BEGAN TO VIBRATE.

LET'S GET BACK TO THE BUSHES.

AT THAT INSTANT I THRUST OUT MY HAND. IT FELT NOTHING. I WAS PLUNGING INTO A BOTTOMLESS HOLE!

CAVOR GRIPPED MY LEGS AND PULLED ME BACK.

WE SCRAMBLED FRANTICALLY TO SOLID GROUND.

WHAT HAPPENED?

THAT FLAT AREA WAS NO MORE THAN A GIGANTIC LID. IT OPENED SUDDENLY AND YOU ALMOST WENT INTO THE PIT.

WE CREPT CLOSER AND PEERED INTO THE BLACKNESS.

THE SELENITES MUST LIVE IN THESE CAVERNS DURING THE NIGHT AND COME OUT DURING THE DAY.

I'D LIKE TO KNOW MORE, BUT WE DARE RISK NOTHING UNTIL WE FIND THE SPHERE.

IF WE DO NOT FIND IT SOON, I WILL DIE OF HUNGER.

SUDDENLY OUR NEED FOR FOOD BECAME OVERPOWERING.

THIS MUSHROOM-LIKE THING LOOKS EDIBLE.

WE BROKE OFF PIECES AND STUFFED THEM IN OUR MOUTHS.

IT'S GOOD!

IN A FEW MINUTES MY HEAD BEGAN TO SWIM. CAVOR WAS STAGGERING.

IT HAS MADE US DRUNK!

IN A DAZE I BECAME AWARE THAT SOME OF THE ANT-LIKE CREATURES WERE STARING AT US. THEN ALL WAS DARKNESS.

WE AWOKE IN A SORT OF CAVERN. I TRIED TO RAISE MY HANDS TO MY ACHING HEAD, BUT FOUND THEY WERE CHAINED TOGETHER.

CAVOR, WHY AM I BOUND?

THE SELENITES -- THE MOON PEOPLE HAVE DONE IT.

THEY'VE GOT US, THEN!

WE SAT MUSING FOR A WHILE.

WHERE DO YOU THINK WE ARE?

PROBABLY IN A CAVERN INSIDE THE MOON. IT'S COOLER HERE, AND THE AIR IS DENSER.

SUDDENLY...

LOOK AT THAT BLUE LIGHT.

A DOOR IS OPENING!

SILHOUETTED IN THE DOOR STOOD A GROTESQUE LOOKING CREATURE.

HE STOOD GAZING AT US SILENTLY FOR A FEW MINUTES.

THEN HE TURNED AND DISAPPEARED.

WHAT DO YOU MAKE OF THAT?

THEY ARE MORE HUMAN THAN WE HAD A RIGHT TO EXPECT.

THE PROBLEM IS COMMUNICATION. THEY MUST HAVE INTELLIGENCE FOR THEY MAKE THINGS -- THAT LID, FOR INSTANCE.

AND THEY MUST HAVE SOME IDEA OF MERCY, OR THEY WOULD HAVE KILLED US AT ONCE.

OUR CONVERSATION WAS CUT OFF BY THE APPEARANCE OF SEVERAL MORE SELENITES CARRYING BOWLS.

IT LOOKS LIKE FOOD.

SEE, THEY KNOW WE MAY BE HUNGRY.

WE ATE RAVENOUSLY. WHEN WE HAD FINISHED, THEY LOOSENED OUR BONDS AND MOTIONED FOR US TO GET UP.

GUARDED BY FOUR GOAD-BEARING SELENITES, WE EMERGED FROM OUR CHAMBER INTO A MUCH LARGER CAVERN.

LOOK AT THAT -- A MACHINE FOR MAKING LIQUID LIGHT!

INDEED! AND IT SEEMS THE LIGHT IS CHANNELLED INTO GUTTERS WHICH RUN FROM CAVERN TO CAVERN.

WE WALKED FOR SOME TIME. FINALLY WE REACHED WHAT SEEMED TO BE THE EDGE OF A CLIFF. A NARROW PLANK PROJECTED FROM IT INTO THE VOID.

I THINK THEY WANT US TO WALK ON THAT PLANK.

IT'S QUITE IMPOSSIBLE. THEY CAN'T KNOW WHAT IT IS TO BE DIZZY.

AS WE STOOD THERE STUBBORNLY REFUSING TO MOVE, ONE OF THE GUARDS PRICKED ME WITH HIS GOAD.

I SWUNG AROUND IN A FURY.

CONFOUND YOU, WHAT DO YOU THINK I'M MADE OF, TO STICK THAT INTO ME?

MY ANGER RELEASED SOME RESERVE STORE OF ENERGY, AND WITH A WRENCH, I SNAPPED MY CHAINS.

I STRUCK THE GUARD AND SENT HIM SPINNING.

HOW FLIMSY HE WAS!

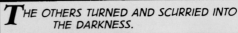

THE OTHERS TURNED AND SCURRIED INTO THE DARKNESS.

I BROKE THE CHAIN ABOUT MY ANKLES. THEN I BROKE CAVOR'S CHAINS.

THERE, WE'RE FREE. LET'S GET OUT OF HERE.

WE SET OFF IN BIG LEAPS BY THE PATH WE HAD COME.

WE HEARD A TUMULT OF SOUNDS ADVANCING ON US AS WE MADE A BOLT FOR THE SIDE CAVERN.

*B*UT IT WAS NOT DAYLIGHT AFTER ALL.

IT'S COMING THROUGH THIS GRATING.

LISTEN -- THERE ARE SELENITES UP THERE!

IT SOUNDS AS IF THEY ARE OCCUPIED WITH SOME SORT OF WORK. IF I CAN BEND THIS GRATING, WE CAN PULL OURSELVES UP AND SEE.

I BENT THE BARS EASILY, AND PRESENTLY CAVOR AND I WERE LYING SIDE BY SIDE IN THE DEPRESSION IN WHICH THE GRATING LAY.

*W*E CAUTIOUSLY PEERED OVER THE EDGE.

THERE, LYING IN A LINE, WERE THE IMMENSE CARCASSES OF MOON-CALVES, AND AROUND THEM A BUSY BAND OF MOON-BUTCHERS.

WE LAY WATCHING IN SILENCE. THEN...

SOMETHING'S COMING UP FROM BELOW!

SUDDENLY A SPEAR FLASHED UP AT US!

I CAUGHT IT AND BEGAN JABBING DOWN AT THE SQUEALING SELENITES.

*T*HEN AN AXE HURTLED THROUGH THE AIR FROM THE CAVERN.

IT'S THE MOON-BUTCHERS! GUARD THE GRATING, CAVOR! I'LL TRY TO STAND THEM OFF.

*B*UT AS I RUSHED TO MEET THEM, THEY TURNED AND FLED A LITTLE WAY UP THE SLOPE.

I FOLLOWED THEM TO THE FIRST CARCASS, WHERE I SPOTTED TWO HEAVY CROWBARS.

NOW HERE ARE DECENT WEAPONS!

I TURNED BACK TO CAVOR. HE WAS RUNNING TOWARDS ME.

GO BACK! WHAT ARE YOU DOING?

THEY'VE GOT -- IT'S LIKE A GUN!

THERE WAS A SELENITE AIMING AN APPARATUS THAT LOOKED LIKE A CROSSBOW.

AS I LEAPED AT HIM, I FELT A SPEAR GO INTO MY SHOULDER.

I WRENCHED IT OUT AND BEGAN TO JAB DOWN THE GRATING WITH IT.

*F*INALLY I HURLED IT DOWN.

LET'S TRY TO GET OUT THROUGH THE CAVERN.

*W*E TURNED AND RAN TOWARDS THE MOON-BUTCHERS. THEY WERE JOINED BY MORE SELENITES CARRYING SPEARS.

*T*HEY IMMEDIATELY LET LOOSE A VOLLEY.

IF WE GET BEHIND THE CARCASSES OF THE MOON-CALVES, WE CAN WORK OUR WAY UP THE CAVE.

*W*HEN WE GOT TO THE LAST CARCASS...

WE MUST MAKE A RUN FOR IT NOW.

*S*WINGING RIGHT AND LEFT, WE HURTLED THROUGH THE FLIMSY MOON-PEOPLE IN VAST, FLYING STRIDES.

*L*EAVING THEM BEHIND, WE RAN UP THE TUNNEL AND EMERGED, AT LAST, INTO THE SUNLIGHT OF THE SURFACE.

WORN OUT, WE SAT DOWN TO REST. I GLANCED AT THE CROWBARS WE STILL CARRIED.

WHY, THEY'RE MADE OF GOLD!

AND THE CHAINS, TOO. IT MUST BE A VERY COMMON METAL HERE.

WE COULD BE RICH! WHEN WE COME BACK...

COME BACK? NO, ASSUMING WE ARE LUCKY ENOUGH TO GET HOME, I DO NOT THINK I WOULD COME AGAIN.

IF OUR SECRET GOT OUT, GOVERNMENTS AND MEN WOULD STRUGGLE TO GET HERE. THEY WOULD FIGHT AGAINST ONE ANOTHER AND AGAINST THESE MOON-PEOPLE. THIS PLANET WOULD SOON BE STREWN WITH DEAD.

IT IS NOT AS THOUGH MAN HAD ANY USE FOR THE MOON. EVEN OF HIS OWN PLANET, WHAT HAS HE MADE BUT A BATTLE GROUND AND THEATRE OF INFINITE FOLLY?

PERHAPS YOU'RE RIGHT. BUT IF WE EXPECT EVER TO GET TO EARTH AGAIN, WE'D BETTER START LOOKING FOR THE SPHERE.

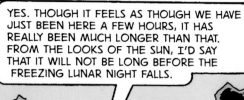

YES. THOUGH IT FEELS AS THOUGH WE HAVE JUST BEEN HERE A FEW HOURS, IT HAS REALLY BEEN MUCH LONGER THAN THAT. FROM THE LOOKS OF THE SUN, I'D SAY THAT IT WILL NOT BE LONG BEFORE THE FREEZING LUNAR NIGHT FALLS.

LET'S HOIST THIS HANDKERCHIEF AS A MARKER AND WORK SEPARATELY AROUND IT.

VERY WELL. IF ONE OF US COMES UPON THE SPHERE, HE MUST COME BACK TO THE MARKER AND SIGNAL TO THE OTHER.

AND IF NEITHER...?

WE GO ON SEEKING UNTIL THE NIGHT AND COLD OVERTAKE US.

WE SAID GOODBYE, AND CAVOR LEAPED OFF, LEAVING ME QUITE ALONE ON THIS STRANGE MOON WORLD.

THE COLD EVENING AIR REMINDED ME THAT TIME WAS SHORT.

NOW WHERE CAN CAVOR BE?

LEAVING MY GOLD CROWBARS IN THE SPHERE, I SET OFF TOWARDS THE THICKET WHERE THE HANDKERCHIEF FLUTTERED.

CAVOR! CAVOR!

BUT THERE WAS NO SIGN OF HIM.

THEN...

WHY, HERE'S CAVOR'S CAP! AND THAT LITTLE PIECE OF PAPER LOOKS LIKE A NOTE.

I SEIZED IT EAGERLY.

They have been chasing me, and it is only a question of time before they get me. I can hear them coming closer. I intend—

THE NOTE ENDED ABRUPTLY.

POOR CAVOR! THAY HAVE GOTTEN HIM. I AM ALONE.

*A*S I STOOD THERE, SOMETHING VERY SOFT AND LIGHT TOUCHED MY HAND.

A SNOWFLAKE! THE NIGHT IS FALLING!

*I*N A FRENZY, I STARTED FOR THE SPHERE.

SHALL I REACH IT IN TIME? AH, HEAVEN, SHALL I REACH IT?

I STRUGGLED NUMBLY ON. I FELL AND CRAWLED ON ALL FOURS.

*F*INALLY I WAS THERE. THE SNOW FELL ALL ABOUT ME AS I PULLED MYSELF IN.

I SCREWED THE MANHOLE COVER INTO PLACE AND FUMBLED WITH THE SWITCHES. SOMETHING CLICKED, AND IN AN INSTANT I WAS IN THE SILENCE AND DARKNESS OF INTER-PLANETARY SPACE.

I DO NOT KNOW HOW LONG I DRIFTED AIMLESSLY. THEN...

I'D BETTER TRY TO GET MY BEARINGS.

I OPENED A BLIND AND GOT A GLIMPSE OF THE EARTH.

I'M GOING IN THE RIGHT DIRECTION.

A FTER A JOURNEY OF WHAT MAY HAVE BEEN WEEKS, I FOUND MYSELF SWIFTLY DROPPING TO EARTH.

I OPENED ALL THE BLINDS AND LANDED IN THE OCEAN WITH A TREMENDOUS SPLASH.

A FEW MINUTES LATER, I WAS ROCKING UPON THE SURFACE OF THE SEA. MY JOURNEY IN SPACE WAS AT AN END.

OH, YES. WERE YOU CAST AWAY OR SOMETHING?

YES. WOULD YOU HELP ME GET SOME STUFF UP ON THE BEACH?

HELP? OF COURSE! WHAT PARTICULARLY DO YOU WANT DONE?

THERE ARE TWO BIG BARS OF GOLD IN THAT SPHERE THAT I WOULD LIKE CARRIED TO THE HOTEL.

HE STARED AT ME INCREDULOUSLY AS I PULLED THEM OUT.

I SAY, WHERE DID YOU GET THOSE?

I'LL TELL YOU WHEN I'VE HAD SOME FOOD.

SEVERAL OTHER MEN CAME BY AND WE ENLISTED THEIR AID. AS WE WENT ALONG, I SAW A SMALL BOY CYCLING IN THE DIRECTION OF THE SPHERE.

DON'T WORRY. HE WON'T TOUCH IT.

THUS REASSURED, WE CONTINUED TO THE HOTEL, WHERE I ORDERED A LARGE BREAKFAST.

BUT WHERE DID YOU GET THE GOLD?

WELL, I GOT IT ON THE MOON.

SEE HERE, WE'RE NOT GOING TO BELIEVE THAT, YOU KNOW.

JUST THEN THERE CAME A NOISE LIKE THE FIRING OF A TREMENDOUS ROCKET.

WHAT'S THAT?

IT'S THAT BOY -- THAT ACCURSED BOY!

I RUSHED TO THE BEACH. THERE WAS NO SIGN OF THE SPHERE.

HE'S MEDDLED WITH THE BLINDS AND GONE UP! NOW I SHALL NEVER BE ABLE TO GO BACK!

I DEPOSITED MY GOLD IN A BANK, WROTE AND PUBLISHED THE STORY OF MY JOURNEY AND CONSIDERED MY ADVENTURE AT AN END. BUT SEVERAL MONTHS LATER, I RECEIVED A LETTER FROM A DUTCH SCIENTIST, MR. JULIUS WENDIGEE.

THIS IS INCREDIBLE!

ON APPARATUS HE HAS DESIGNED, HE IS GETTING FRAGMENTARY MESSAGES IN ENGLISH FROM THE MOON!

I HURRIED TO HIS OBSERVATORY.

IT MUST BE CAVOR! ARE THE MESSAGES STILL COMING IN?

YES. SO FAR HE HAS SAID THAT HE IS ALIVE AND WELL, AND IS ALLOWED A GREAT DEAL OF FREEDOM.

HE HAS DESCRIBED A GREAT LUNAR SEA AND THE IMMENSE NETWORK OF CAVERNS IN THE MOON. HE HAS ALSO DESCRIBED THE PEOPLE. AH, HERE IS ANOTHER MESSAGE COMING IN.

TODAY I SAW THE GRAND LUNAR, THE MASTER OF THE MOON. THESE SELENITES ARE VERY CLEVER. THEY HAVE LEARNED TO DECIPHER MY LANGUAGE SO WE ARE ABLE TO TALK.

THE GRAND LUNAR ASKED ME MANY QUESTIONS ABOUT MEN. I TOLD HIM ABOUT OUR GOVERNMENTS AND I TOLD HIM ABOUT WAR.

THAT'S ALL I CAN GET NOW. THERE'S TOO MUCH INTERFERENCE.

CAVOR IS A FOOL! HE HAS TALKED OF WAR AND VIOLENCE. HE HAS FILLED THE WHOLE MOON-WORLD WITH THIS IMPRESSION OF OUR RACE, WHEN IT IS PLAIN TO THEM THAT UPON HIMSELF ALONE HANGS THE POSSIBILITY OF OTHER MEN REACHING THE MOON.

THEN SUDDENLY, LIKE A CRY IN THE NIGHT, CAME THE LAST MESSAGE.

I WAS MAD TO LET THE GRAND LUNAR KNOW...

THAT WAS THE LAST MESSAGE FROM CAVOR. AFTER IT WAS ONLY A SILENCE THAT HAS NO END.

THE END

Tales of the Moon

There have been many tales of voyages to the Moon in Western literature.

In 1638 Francis Godwin published a book entitled *The Man in the Moon*, which tells of an explorer who trains a flock of geese to tow an aerial carriage to the Moon. Daniel Defoe, best known as the author of *Robinson Crusoe*, wrote a 1705 novel called *The Consolidator*, in which a ship travels to the Moon powered by magical spirits. A pseudonymous 1728 satire called *A Trip to the Moon* described a lunar voyage that is propelled by gunpowder - a better guess than any other early writer made. But most tales of voyages into space were still essentially fairy tales or satires.

It was only in the 19th Century, when the Industrial Revolution was demonstrating that mechanical inventions could perform wonders, that some writers began to treat voyages into space with a degree of scientific accuracy.

Joseph Atterley's 1827 novel *A Voyage to the Moon* may be the first lunar adventure that could be called "science fiction" rather than "fantasy," as Atterley's tale is told in a spirit of scientific speculation. Atterley's space ship, however, like Wells' Sphere in *The First Men in the Moon*, is powered simply by an anti-gravity metal. Edgar Allan Poe's 1835 story *The Unparalleled Adventure of One Hans Pfall* uses a balloon filled with an imaginary gas lighter than hydrogen. Poe's carefully described voyage of a trip in a balloon seems to be the first story that actually made an attempt to describe how such a journey might be possible. Hans Pfall carefully calculates how long it will take him to reach the Moon at a speed of sixty miles an hour, and takes into account the fact that the higher one ascends from the Earth, the thinner the atmosphere becomes. Poe got a number of things wrong, but his attempt at scientific authenticity was unsurpassed until Jules Verne tried his hand thirty years later, with his *From the Earth to the Moon*.

Although none of these writers suggest rocket power as a means to launch a space vehicle, Verne certainly came closest with his gigantic cannon. Verne correctly deduced that a space vehicle would have to attain "escape velocity" - a speed fast enough to escape the Earth's gravitational field - and calculated this speed to be 12,000 yards per second, or more than 24,000 miles per hour. This is, in fact, close to the speed attained by the Apollo missions that flew to the Moon in the 1960s-70s.

Wells joined the long list of writers dealing with lunar voyages in 1901 when he wrote *The First Men in the Moon*. It is one of his many "Scientific Romances" and plays out in a similar style to his *The Time Machine*, with an inventor who creates the means to journey to somewhere fantastic, and who goes on to experience a perilous adventure with a seemingly primitive and hostile underground race.

Frontispiece to *The First Men in the Moon*

Man and the Moon

In 1962 at Rice University, John F. Kennedy set the objective for American scientists to land a man on the Moon before the end of that decade. Some of his words are recalled below as an example of leadership and challenge – of setting a vision and exciting his nation in that pursuit:

"We choose to go to the Moon. We choose to go to the Moon in this decade and do the other things, not because they are easy, but because they are hard, because that goal will serve to organise and measure the best of our energies and skills, because that challenge is one that we are willing to accept, one we are unwilling to postpone, and one which we intend to win, and the others, too.

Many years ago the great British explorer George Mallory, who was to die on Mount Everest, was asked why did he want to climb it. He said, "Because it is there."

Well, space is there, and we're going to climb it, and the Moon and the planets are there, and new hopes for knowledge and peace are there. And, therefore, as we set sail we ask God's blessing on the most hazardous and dangerous and greatest adventure on which man has ever embarked".

The race to meet his goal would require the greatest technological achievement the world has ever seen. The first Apollo missions were spent getting ready for the Moon Landing. Apollo 8 and Apollo 10 even flew all the way to the Moon, around it, and back to Earth. Then, on July 16th, 1969, Apollo 11 launched from Kennedy Space Centre in Florida. They travelled to the Moon and arrived in lunar orbit on July 19th. On July 20th, 1969, Neil Armstrong was the first astronaut to step on the Moon with the unforgettable words "That's one small step for man, one giant leap for mankind". He was soon joined by Buzz Aldrin. The two astronauts spent 21 hours on the Moon doing experiments and taking pictures. They also brought back 46 pounds of moon rocks helping answer many of the geological questions until then unanswered. The whole programme was an extraordinary success – perhaps the greatest exploratory journey achieved by Man, then and still today.

In fact, the "one small step for man" wasn't actually that small. Armstrong set the ship down so gently that its shock absorbers didn't compress. He had to hop three and a half feet from the Eagle's ladder to the surface.

The toughest moonwalk task was planting the flag! NASA's studies suggested that the lunar soil was soft, but Armstrong and Aldrin found the surface to be a thin wisp of dust over hard rock. They managed to drive the flagpole a few inches into the ground and film it for broadcast, and then took care not to accidentally knock it over.

Thus man's fascination with visiting the Moon was accomplished just 68 years after *The First Men in the Moon* was published. Wells had foreseen that one day man would conquer that frontier.

John Fitzgerald Kennedy (1917 - 1963)

The First Men in the Moon in Film

As with most novels of its age, *The First Men in the Moon* has been adapted for film several times.

The first adaptation was jointly adapted from Jules Verne's *From the Earth to the Moon*, and used elements from both novels to construct its plot. This was master-dreamweaver Georges Méliès' *Le Voyage dans La Lune* (*A Trip to the Moon*), made in 1902.

One of the earliest of all narrative films, this version ran for only 14 minutes, but has since been considered one of the greatest science fiction films ever made, pioneering film technique beyond many people's imaginations at the time.

The cannon prepares to fire
the scientists to the Moon.
A Trip to the Moon (1902)

Méliès has a group of scientists, intent on visiting the Moon, build a cannon to fire themselves in a bullet-shaped shell off the Earth (the cannon was taken from Verne's novel, instead of using the substance "Cavorite" as is the method for leaving Earth in *The First Men in the Moon*). Once on the Moon, the scientists encounter strange, hostile beings who attack them, but are easily defeated with a single touch from an umbrella! The encounter with strange beings is taken from Wells' story.

The film is perhaps at its most iconic with the image of the rocket/bullet landing right in the eye of the man in the Moon.

The Moon is struck by the rocket.
A Trip to the Moon (1902)

In 1919, Wells' novel was adapted in full and on its own for the first time. This version, directed by Bruce Gordon and J. L. V. Leigh has since been lost, and is currently on the British Film Institute's list of "75 Most Wanted" lost films.

A third adaptation was made in 1964. Directed by Nathan H. Juran, this version begins with a 1964 space exploration to the Moon, believed to be the first, discovering a British flag already there with a note which leads them to the elderly Arnold Bedford, who, in flashback, tells the tale of his adventure to the Moon with Cavor 65 years earlier.

Theatrical Poster for
The First Men in the Moon directed by
Nathan H. Juran
(Columbia Pictures)

The latest adaptation of the novel was made for BBC TV in 2010, starring Rory Kinnear as Bedford and Mark Gatiss as Cavor. Gatiss wrote the script, which is considered the version which stays most faithful to the novel.